THE TIGER
ON HIS BACK

BERNARD ASHLEY

THE TIGER
ON HIS BACK

Barrington Stoke

First published in 2018 in Great Britain by
Barrington Stoke Ltd
18 Walker Street, Edinburgh, EH3 7LP

www.barringtonstoke.co.uk

A CIP catalogue record for this book is available
from the British Library upon request

ISBN: 978-1-78112-812-1

Printed in China by Leo

CONTENTS

*With huge thanks to tattoo artist
Luke Ashley and to Danny Barratt*

CHAPTER 1
Sofia's secret

"Will it hurt?" Sofia wanted to know.

"'Course it will," her friend Lydia told her.

"What am I doing?!" Sofia asked. Her heart was thumping wildly, because *Help! Here it was!* The Covent Garden Tattoo studio.

Lydia grabbed Sofia's arm. "Come on, animal rights girl! If you want a tiger tattooed on your bum, you've got to suffer for it!"

"I'm not having it on my bum!" Sofia exclaimed.

"Wherever."

Sofia's stomach flipped every time she thought about her tattoo – this secret that would soon be out of her head and inked into her skin. It was something that would be there on her body for the rest of her life – yes, until the day she died.

"Come on, Sofe," Lydia said.

"It's all right for you ..." Sofia hung back.

"This guy's brilliant. If he can light up his colours on me, he'll dazzle away on you."

Lydia was talking about her skin being black while Sofia's was white. But the real difference between them was that Lydia's tattoos didn't have to be secret. Her mum and dad had tattoos and they showed them off, while Sofia's mother pulled a face every time she saw one.

"You're making a *statement*, girl," Lydia said. "An' it's going to be a clear and strong statement about you, Sofia Drake. That's what you told me."

And that was true – it was exactly why Sofia wanted her tattoo. If her exam results were OK, she would go to university in September to study Wildlife Conservation. And her secret tiger's head tattoo would be her promise to herself that she would devote her life to keeping rare animals alive on this earth.

"So, are we going in or not?" Lydia said. Her patience had begun to run out.

Sofia found her tiger spirit. "In. Of course in."

The studio was near Covent Garden Market in an arcade of shops and cafes – all such *painless* places. Lydia led the way inside. The ground floor was for piercing, and Annie, the piercer, told them to go on up to the first floor to find Sol. The stairs were steep, every step asking Sofia, *Are you sure, girl?* They went up to a small landing where an open door showed a tattooing bed with a length of surgical paper on top. Ready for someone. But it wouldn't be Sofia. *No way! Not today!*

"Go in." A man had come out of a room behind them. He was tall, with no piercings or facial tattoos. "You'll have to squeeze up."

"Hiya, Sol." Lydia bounced a bit and seemed very pleased to see him.

"Hi," Sol replied.

"This is Sofe – Sofia," Lydia went on.

Sol shook Sofia's hand. He was a couple of years older than her and wore a baseball cap with a light strapped around it. He threw a pair of disposable gloves into a bin as he followed them into the room with the bed, then waved an arm at a small settee against the wall – an invitation to sit. From speakers in the ceiling, Amy Whitehouse was singing "Tears Dry On Their Own".

"Sofe's dad's a famous actor," Lydia announced.

"*Lydia!*" Sofia groaned.

"Tony Drake. You know, *Murder HQ* on TV." Lydia carried on regardless.

"Sorry, I don't," Sol said. "Overdosed on TV as a kid. So ..."

He sat in a swivel chair next to the bed. "You tell me what you want," he said to Sofia. His folded arms were tattooed like beautiful works of art, Japanese designs that could have been done on silk. "Lydia said something about a tiger?" he prompted.

Sofia told Sol what she wanted. "A fully grown tiger's head and nothing cuddly. It's got to be defiant and dangerous – not vulnerable as if it's in someone's gunsights."

"Why?" Sol asked.

"Why, what?" Did he want an argument about killing wildlife?

"Why do you want it? What's it for? A badge of belonging? I used to tattoo gangs at another place, all with the same Russian star. Or is it for credibility?"

Sofia stiffened her body in self-defence. This guy really did come to the point! "Yes!" she said. "*My own* credibility."

Sol didn't frown; his face was open, neither friendly nor unfriendly.

"It'll remind me of what I'm about when things get hard," she went on. "Exams, people, tricky situations."

Sol nodded. "So where do you want this badge? Do you want to display it?"

"No – it's just for me," Sofia explained. "It needs to be somewhere ... *discreet*."

"Discreet ... Do you mean secret? If you do, a good place is the outside of the leg, high up." Sol's

5

voice was as matter-of-fact as a doctor's. "It's not too tender there and it can be hidden beneath your clothes."

Sofia wanted time to think but Sol stood up – the meeting was over. "Give me your phone number, I'll send you a couple of designs and we'll go from there. I'll tell you the price, book you in and I'll do it in one session. And don't forget your passport. I need to see proof that you're over eighteen." He had recited his list like the end of a radio advert. Then he looked her right in the eye. "So why's your tattoo a secret? Wouldn't your parents be proud of your commitment to wildlife?"

Sofia was ready for this. "They are – but they'd rather they saw it in a picture frame." Talk of her parents made her stomach churn again. Now she had to go home and start telling the lie of a lifetime. She was good at bending the truth, but this was on another level. And as for saying sorry? No, ma'am!

CHAPTER 2

Good news

Sofia and Lydia unlocked their bikes in the station car park as they prepared to go home.

"Sol's a great guy, Sofe," Lydia said. "When you see your tiger, you're gonna be blown away!" – and she freewheeled away. Sofia then pedalled fast up the hill towards her house so she could walk indoors hot and out of breath. Well, she'd told her parents she'd been cycling along the Thames Walk all afternoon, hadn't she?

But she was in for a big surprise. It was a warm Easter and the house windows were open – and had she just heard the pop of a Champagne cork? She had – because she walked in on a full-blown celebration. Her dad had just landed the big film part he'd gone after. Tony Drake was going to play the villain in a new movie with Gloria Gold, the Oscar-winning Hollywood star.

"Isn't it *fantastico*?" Sofia's mother twirled around the sitting room without spilling a drop of her bubbly. She poured a glass for Sofia, and they clinked. Sofia lifted her glass to toast her dad, who was sitting on the settee with a strange look on his face. Pleased? Dazed? Ready to throw up? It was hard to tell. But her mother, Adriana Angeli, was whooping for Italy.

"Gloria Gold! Waterside Films! You'll be up there with the best, Tonio. Right up there!"

Tony Drake was beginning to be known on TV as a regular character on *Murder HQ*, a Sky police series, and Sofia was always pleased when someone recognised him in the street. Now, after a big part in a Gloria Gold film, he'd be recognised in America as well.

"Well done, Tony!" Sofia called her father Tony, while her mother was Ma, an Italian mamma. Sofia went over to Tony now and plonked herself on his lap, spilling his drink.

"Thanks very much, kid."

She gave him a sip from her own glass and took his for her mother to refill it. But just as she held it out to her ma, her phone blipped. She took a quick look – and Ma missed.

"Hold it steady, girl!" her ma cried.

"Sorry," said Sofia.

It was an email from Sol. "What's up with Lyd now?" Sofia said, for her parents' sake, and headed up to her room to open it.

"What do you think of this?"

And there was her tiger, with brilliant markings and riveting eyes staring out at her – fearless and fierce and ready to pounce. It told a story, just looking at it. *Brilliant! Wonderful! Magnifico!* Sol had got it just right. There was something special about the image, although she didn't know exactly what. She would feel so proud every time she looked at this masterpiece! Sol must have had it in his portfolio, because he wouldn't have had time to design something as good as this. This was a true work of art.

She texted him.

"It's great Sol! Thanks. Absolutely right.
Are you inside my head?"

"No, just mine. How about Tuesday.
1 p.m.? Someone's let me down."

Help! Tuesday! Her tattoo, so soon! Sofia's
insides started to churn. This was getting
serious. It was going to happen. She texted back
and went downstairs again. As she walked in, Ma
was saying, "Here's to *The Tiger On His Back!*"

"What's that?" Sofia asked.

"The name of the film!" Ma answered.

"Really?"

As Sofia held out her glass for a wee drop
more Champagne, all she could hear in her head
was, *And here's to the tiger on my leg!*

CHAPTER 3

The business!

On Tuesday, Sofia went to Sol's studio on her own. Lydia was a great friend but this appointment was between her and Sol and the tiger.

It had been easy to get out of the house – her mother designed costumes for stage and TV and had gone to the National Theatre, while her father had an early call for *Murder HQ*. Sofia rode her bike to the station and took the train to Charing Cross and Covent Garden Tattoo. During the journey, she kept thinking how things felt much more serious when they were about *you*. Today wasn't about *a tattoo*, it was about *her tattoo*. And it was going to hurt …

When she got to the studio, she gave Sol his cash, which he counted, very business-like, and put in a drawer. She showed him her passport and he told her how things would go. He sounded so relaxed that it made her nervous.

Sol then said, "I'll shave the tattoo area first, so the needle can't push a tiny hair inwards and cause infection. Then on goes the tiger stencil, which I'll give five minutes to dry—"

"How about five years?" Sofia interrupted.

He ignored this comment. "Just stand by the chair. What sort of music do you like?" he asked.

Sofia didn't know. The last thing she was thinking about was music. "You choose," she said.

"I'll find something instrumental. Peder Helland. No lyrics, easier for me to concentrate."

"Fine," she muttered. The music was fine, yes. But she wasn't.

"Ready?" Sol asked.

"Yes," Sofia croaked.

Sol's cap light was switched on. "Shave first," he said. He sat on his swivel chair, then bent to Sofia's leg and sterilised the tattoo site with alcohol.

"Phew! That's strong!" Sofia gasped.

"Don't smell it myself any more," Sol said as he started with the razor. "You liked my tiger, then?"

"It's superb," she said.

"It wasn't off a standard flash-sheet – what I show to everyone when they're choosing. Your tiger goes way back. I'll tell you about it sometime."

With the non-stop talking and the music in the background, Sofia felt as if she was at the dentist's.

"Now, some Dettol …" Sol warned.

The antiseptic was cold.

"And on goes the stencil, so stay still," he ordered.

Sofia could feel him stretch her skin and press the stencil on. He rubbed it in, held it there for a while, and pulled it off. She felt every move – so if she was as sensitive as this to things on the surface, what would it be like when the needle went in?

"Look down here," Sol said. He was holding a magnifying mirror to show her the stencil outline of the tiger on her leg. "There it is."

Sofia stared at it. But it was only an outline and hard to make out.

"Ready to go ahead?" Sol asked.

Sofia took a deep breath. She'd got this far, so the answer had to be yes. "Yup," she managed.

"OK," Sol said. "Tell me anytime you want me to stop."

Sofia just growled.

And it did hurt, this attack on her skin by a sharp needle. Her whole body flinched in self-defence. It was like being pinched hard without any let-up – by hot, sharp fingernails that stabbed deep into her over and over again. One spasm of pain merged into another spasm of pain. She wanted to cry out to Sol to give it a break, to stop – but she wouldn't let herself do that. She stared at the wall, her eyes feeling dry in their sockets. Her lips hurt from keeping her mouth shut so tightly. She breathed in, then held it, before letting the air burst out. And all the while she grated, *Mamma! Mamma! Mamma! Mamma!* so deep down in her throat that it burned.

How was she going to get through this? The tattooing went on and on and it hurt, hurt, hurt. She wanted it to stop but she wouldn't admit it – and after ten minutes of deep agony, little by little the pain seemed to soften and her breathing started to return to normal. *Had this been the worst of it, or would it all start up again*, she wondered.

Thank god it didn't get any worse. Sol told her that first pain had been caused by his outlining machine, and after a break for both of them he changed to his shading machine.

Sol took breaks to clean his needles and change his ink colours, and all in all it took almost two hours until the buzzing of the machine stopped and didn't restart.

Mamma mia! The relief! Sofia unclenched her fists and relaxed her jaw.

Sol dabbed and wiped the tattoo site, then pulled out his magnifying mirror again for Sofia to look at her tiger.

As soon as Sofia saw the finished tattoo, her pain was forgotten. "It's fantastic, Sol! It's just what I wanted! More than!" Tears welled up. "And I love its blue eyes."

Sol smiled. "That's where I cheated," he said.

"Cheated?" she asked.

"Most tigers have yellow eyes; only white tigers have blue," Sol told her.

"But this isn't a white tiger ..." Sofia stared into the mirror again. "It's filled with colour."

"Which makes your tiger unique. And a cheat!"

Sol took the mirror away and put Vaseline and cling film over the tattoo. "Take this off after a couple of hours but keep the site moist with Savlon," he instructed.

Sofia felt as if she was high in the sky, filled with pride and with daring.

"That's it, then. You can go," Sol told her.

"Thank you, Sol!" Sofia went to the door. Her beautiful tiger was part of her now. She could feel it hot on the side of her leg. Sofia felt emotional and she very nearly kissed Sol on the cheek.

"There's just that one thing I want to know," he said.

"Yes?"

Sol folded his arms. "How come a bright, determined girl like you, who knows where she's going and what her life's going to be all about ..."

Oh, no! Sofia knew where this was leading. What a persistent man!

"How come she hasn't got the courage to tell her parents that it's *her* body, that *she* owns it – and if she wants a tattoo she's going to have one?" Sol's eyes opened wide with the question. "Because I'd have thought Sofia Drake would be up to that – someone who was really scared of being tattooed but took it like a hero."

"Well, that's my business, isn't it?" Sofia said.

"Yup. Sorry." He looked her in the eyes. "But you need to know you're not the only one. We've all had our struggles with our parents."

"I guess," Sofia said. And she walked out of the room and went very carefully down Sol's steep stairs.

CHAPTER 4
Left turn

Back at school, Easter was over and Sofia's tiger was still shining out on her leg like a polished badge. Lydia and the girls in her tutor group loved it.

"What's his name, your little tiger? Blue Eyes?"

Sofia had problems with this. "How do you know it's a he?" she asked. "And why should wild animals have cosy names? I'm not some softy on *Spring Watch*."

"Male or female, it's beautiful. Shame it can't be seen," one of the girls said.

And that was another problem for Sofia. Sol had said it, and now these girls were implying it too: she was ducking the big issue by having her tattoo in a hidden place. Like them, she was over eighteen but she was acting like a fourth-former, scared of what her mum and dad would say, and that was getting to her. The college treated her like an adult but she was acting like a kid, afraid to face up to her parents over her tattoo.

Meanwhile, the tiger became more and more a part of her – and she learned more about it. It was female, Sofia had decided, and solitary like all tigers. And if the tiger were real, she'd be living by her wits and her hunting skills. A look at those fierce blue eyes said how brave the tiger was – which was what Sofia Drake was lacking. The guts to be herself.

So, after two weeks of tying her dressing gown tight and keeping her bedroom door shut, feeling full of self-doubt and self-loathing, Sofia made up her mind that she had to do it. She couldn't go on like this. She had to tell Tony and Ma about her tattoo.

She took them both by surprise over plates of tagliatelle carbonara. The situation wasn't ideal, because Tony had come in from filming and didn't seem too pleased about something. But Sofia decided it was now or never.

"I've got a tattoo," she said.

Tony spluttered over his food.

"*What? Madonna santa!*" Ma sat bolt upright. "*A tattoo?* Not a real one, Sofia?" she said in disbelief.

"A real one."

"Don't joke. Say it's something painted for the summer revue." Her mother's voice had an edge to it.

"Have a look," Sofia said, and she stood up and showed them.

Ma took one look, said "You little fool!" and stormed out of the room. Tony looked long and hard. Then he lifted his eyes to meet hers, and Sofia fought not to look away.

"It's a true work of art, kiddo, whatever the medium."

"I'm sorry, Tony," Sofia said. "But you know my reason for it? My commitment to wildlife ..."

"I do."

"And can you understand it?" she asked.

"Yup, I understand it. So will Ma. Give her time," Tony said.

"I'm not having it removed or anything like that."

"I wouldn't want you to," Tony said. "It's about *your* life, not ours. And it is your body."

He was being so nice that Sofia wanted to cry – but she wouldn't. No, she wouldn't!

Her dad was muttering softly now, like he did when he was solving a crossword with her. "You know, Sofia," he said. "That tiger might just be the answer ..."

"To what?" Sofia knew he had some problem on his mind.

Tony sat back, folded his arms and told her. "My image for the film. I had a costume fitting today – and it was a disaster."

"Oh, I'm sorry," Sofia said.

"The suit and the golf jacket are all right but you should see what they've got for me underneath," he grumbled.

"No sharp shirt?" Sofia asked.

"Under that," Tony replied.

"A string vest?"

"No, the tattoo," he groaned. "I'm 'the man with the tiger on his back', and known for it. Hard. Feared. A legend. But they've given me a fake tattoo of this old pussycat that looks as if it's about to fall out of its tree. All wrong."

He explained to Sofia how it worked. He would have the "tattoo" painted on his back in special make-up that just needed to be touched up each morning.

"When I see yours," Tony went on, "I realise how naff mine is. It just doesn't work."

And this was when Sofia had a bright thought. "Have mine!" she told him. She pulled out her phone to remind him what it looked like. There it was, Sol's tiger. "It's fierce and dangerous – and one of a kind with those blue eyes."

Tony's face lit up. "That … is … a … fantastic … idea!" He spaced the words out slowly – and Sofia knew he was really impressed.

"Do you think your tattoo man would let me use it?" he asked her.

"We can only ask him," Sofia said.

"Then let's do so, kiddo." Tony sat back as if the idea had been his. "Let's see what the man says ..."

CHAPTER 5
Tiger, tiger

Sofia wasn't sure it would be easy to convince Sol about her plan. But she booked an appointment at Covent Garden Tattoo and took Tony with her.

"I've come to ask for your help," Tony told Sol as they went for a coffee next door. "The thing is, Waterside Films are the bosses. They can *force* me to have their rotten tiger on my back – but I bet I could sell them on yours. It's brilliant. It's got a rare, fierce beauty."

"So if they wanted it, someone would paint my tiger on your back?" Sol asked.

"That's right. With your permission," Tony said.

"And I wouldn't have to be there?"

"No – it'd be copied from a good print by a first-rate make-up artist," Tony confirmed.

"And they'll pay for it?"

"Mega-bucks," Tony told him – and went on to say how the film would sell all over the world, with Sol's name in the credits.

"I see," Sol said.

Tony Drake got up to pay the bill.

"Nice guy, your dad," Sol told Sofia. "Wish I'd had one like that."

Sofia didn't know what to say to that, so she just patted the back of Sol's hand.

"Anyhow, thanks, Sofe," he said. "If it helps you and your dad, it can't do me any harm, can it?"

Sofia somehow kept her face straight as she tried to hide her excitement. "Great!" she said. It was a yes for Tony – but, more than that, Sol had just called her "Sofe". Well, well, well!

*

Things worked out OK at first. The Waterside producer really liked Sol's tiger and made him a very generous offer, so Tony Drake started filming with the blue-eyed tiger on his back. Meanwhile, Sofia decided she'd like a red panda tattoo on her other leg. Well, red pandas were an endangered species too, and it would balance things up. She rang Sol, who said he'd sketch out a couple of designs – and he called her "Sofe" again.

But before she got to see any of Sol's ideas, Tony Drake was on television in a publicity "promo" for *The Tiger on His Back*. She saw it at home with Tony and Ma – an ordinary item on local TV all about Gloria Gold, with a shirtless Tony Drake in the background.

"*Here I am at the side of the River Thames,*" the reporter said, "*and here with me is none other than Hollywood's twenty-four carat Oscar-winning star, Gloria Gold – filming in Britain for the very first time ...*"

Gloria Gold gushed about her role but when she was asked about the title of the film she brought in her co-star. "Turn round, Tony darling," she told him. And he did so – to show off Sol's stunning tiger. It filled the whole of his back and looked ready to leap off it. "And here's the tiger itself," Gloria said.

"Designed by Sol Marks," Tony added, but that was it. The TV producer said, "Cut." It had all been about Gloria Gold and the tiger.

"Huh!" Sofia's mother sounded disappointed as she switched off the TV.

"I've got tomorrow's scenes to learn," Tony said, and went upstairs.

But Sofia was pleased. Her dad was a terrific actor and he'd get some great reviews when the film opened. Meanwhile, he'd given Sol a name check, and that wouldn't do him any harm, would it?

CHAPTER 6

"Tiger" Doolan

Flip Mason was in his tattoo parlour, Living Ink, down in Gravesend, clearing up after a late finish. His wall-sized TV was switched on to keep him company and suddenly one of the images caught his eye. "That's mine!" he shouted at the sight of a tiger on a man's back. "That's on Tiger Doolan's back! He'll kill me!"

Tiger Doolan was a heavyweight boxer, meaty and heavy. Flip had tattooed the tiger on his back for the biggest fight of his life – at the Royal Albert Hall when he'd won the British belt. It was his trademark – and Flip had promised him no one else in the world would ever carry that tiger.

"God, what the hell have you done to me?" Flip yelled, and he scooped up the remote and threw it at the TV as he switched it off. "If Tiger sees that, he'll come in here and tear the place apart." He sat on a chair, like someone waiting. Which he was. Waiting for an idea, for a way out.

"What the hell do I say to Tiger?" he muttered to himself. Tiger was the man who'd told him "I'll kill you if I ever see some other schmuck with my tiger on his back! This is my trademark now – a tiger with blue eyes like mine!" He had poked two fingers at his own face as he spoke. "You gotta swear to me no other geezer will ever have that tiger on his back or anywhere else!" And Flip had made that promise.

Flip's head was in his hands, so he didn't see it at first – the answer that was sitting there across from him, up on the counter near the door. A big old-fashioned cash register he'd bought at Camden Market as a feature for his shop. Now he looked up and saw it. "Money!" he said to himself. "Always on about his *purse*, is Tiger." A man who regularly had his face bashed in for profit would soon settle if it was for a big enough purse. And maybe he'd even be willing to help Flip get his hands on the money. Bound to be, for big bucks.

Sol Marks picked up the phone to an abusive but familiar voice – Flip Mason's. Sol had started work as an apprentice in Living Ink soon after he left school, when he'd had enough of his boozy father and found a place to live with a cousin in Gravesend. This cousin was into tattooing and put him in touch with Flip Mason, who'd been at Living Ink for a year or so, number two to the boss. But after eighteen months Sol had moved back to London, and he'd almost forgotten that whining voice.

"Saw the news," Flip said. "Saw my tiger on some actor's back, and Tiger Doolan's gonna know about it from someone soon enough. And Tiger's a big tasty boxer. He'll make mincemeat of anyone who disrespects him – which means me and it means you!"

"Hold on, hold on," Sol said. "What's this Tiger Doolan got to do with me?"

"He's got my tiger on his back, and so has this actor, done by you. Doolan's not going to like that. Not one little bit." There was a pause before Flip said, "But I reckon I can buy him off for twenty grand."

Sol didn't get the chance to say anything as Flip continued, "I don't give a flyin' turd whether it's you or the film people who pay it. But one of you's goin' to, you can count on that. Or else! I've got a good lawyer an' 'e's just *dribblin'* to get onto my case."

"That's my design and you know it, Mason," Sol said. "Where'd you find it? In with the inks I left behind?"

"It's been in my flash for yonks, Marks, an' you can't prove it hasn't. So you pay up proper or you're gonna regret it, son – big time. Think about it!" And Flip shut off his phone before Sol got a chance to respond.

*

This was only the start. Flip then made the same threats to Waterside Films, and soon afterwards Waterside were on to Sol.

"We've heard from a guy who claims ownership of your tiger design, and we'll take you to court and back, buddy, if you're not the original artist. We've shot too much of the movie to change anything – so you'd better buy this guy off!"

"And have a nice day yourself," Sol said. "I said that's my design and I stand by it."

The worst of the situation was the personal problems it caused – the fallings-out between Waterside Films and Tony Drake, and between Tony Drake and both Sofia and Sol. It was a rotten mess all round, and Sofia went about with the feeling in her stomach she had when exams were coming up. She had to do something about it.

*

The next Saturday Sofia went to Covent Garden Tattoo and waited downstairs until Sol was free. She had to wait for an hour, but at last a big, tough-faced man with a teardrop tattooed on his cheek came down the stairs. Sol followed him part way to call Sofia up.

"He looked a tough one," she said.

"I used to tattoo him in a different parlour. Now he won't have anyone else," Sol explained.

"What's the teardrop about?" Sofia asked.

"Different things to different people. Grief, or a killing." Sol sounded very matter-of-fact.

"Oh, my god!" Sofia said.

"It could be bravado. There's a lot of false bravery when people see the needle," Sol explained.

They were sitting on his settee. Sofia turned to him. "Sol, I'm so sorry about everything."

"Girl, you don't know the half of what's going on."

"Then you'd better tell me. I really want to get this mess sorted out. I owe it to my dad, and to myself – and to you," she said.

Sol sat there in silence for a while, then he told her about Flip Mason and Gravesend and his apprentice job at Living Ink, where Flip still worked and was now claiming the tiger as his own design. "But it's not, Sofe – it's mine," Sol said. "The trouble is, I can't prove it."

"How did you get the tattoo … just out of your head?" Sofia liked the sound of "Sofe" again.

"Yes, but in paint, not ink," Sol replied.

"On someone's back or their arm?" Sofia had seen plenty of painted people at festivals and concerts.

"No. On hardboard, as part of my A Level coursework – got me a top grade," he replied. But he said it in a modest voice.

"So what happened to the painting? Did you take it home?" Sofia wanted to know.

"Nope. My dad wouldn't have wanted it in the house. He wasn't that interested in anything I did."

"Didn't *you* want it, then, Sol?" Sofia asked.

"Why would I? I'd got it on my phone. And by then I was well into tattooing." Sol stared at Sofia. "I'm not a Picasso, Sofe. I don't need an art gallery. I've got my work walking around London."

"Got it," she said. He really was a different kind of guy.

"I wasn't going to lug my paintings and portfolio down to Gravesend on the bus." Sol dusted his hands together. "And that's the end of the story."

But Sofia stood up. "Oh no it isn't! Oh no, Sol Marks!" She wasn't going to let him give up so easily.

His eyes were wide as if he wondered what she meant.

"My college keeps any good artwork people don't want," she said. "It's up in the corridors, in the dining hall, all over the place ..."

"So?" asked Sol. He looked as if he didn't see where she was going with this.

"So you're going back to your old college to find out what happened to your painting," she said. "No teacher in their right mind would chuck out a beautiful piece of work like that."

Now Sol looked interested.

"I'll bet you a hundred to one your name and your grades are pasted on the back of the painting – which would be proof!" she said. "And I'll come with you." She shocked herself saying it.

"You and me?" he asked.

"You and me. Why not?" Sofia smiled.

Sol stayed silent. But his face said he couldn't think of any good reason.

CHAPTER 7

Back to college

Flip Mason shut off his phone and swore. He had just found out how much it would cost to start legal action against Sol Marks – and Flip didn't have that sort of money. He made a call to Sol before Sofia had left the studio to go home.

"Listen, Marks, you're in deep trouble, son. You must have got a load of dosh off the film company for that design. So I want enough to buy off Tiger Doolan, *and* a bit more for me – *and* I want it quick."

Sol's voice was low and steady. "You listen to me, Mason. That tiger is *my* design and what *you* want doesn't come into it. I'm going to prove it and you can whistle for your money. So why don't you sit down and do a decent design of your own?"

Flip Mason swore. "Well, you listen to this, scumbag. You'll soon change your mind when I send Tiger Doolan round to see you. Too right you will! He'll soon persuade you to do what's right by me. He's a wild animal, son. I'll let him know where you hang out, an' he'll be after you real soon." He coughed out a laugh. "Classic, innit? Before you're a coupla days older, you're gonna 'ave a gorilla on your back! An' we'll see what sort of artist you are with all your fingers broke!"

Sol switched off his phone and blew out his cheeks. "Are you free on Monday?" he asked Sofia.

"I could be. My timetable's pretty flexible," Sofia replied.

"Can you do what you said?" Sol asked. "Come with me to my old college? A bit of sweet persuasion from you might help."

"It'll be a pleasure." And Sofia smiled at him because she meant it.

*

Monday morning – and Tiger Doolan was revving his red Ducati Monster 1200 motorbike outside Living Ink in Gravesend. His helmet was in his hands as he listened to Flip Mason.

"You've got his shop address – Covent Garden Tattoo, up Covent Garden somewhere. An' you've got where he lives? Greenwich Wharf Street if he's still there – it's where we sent his mail on to."

Doolan nodded and patted the zip on his leather jacket.

"An' I've given you his picture off his Instagram?" Flip asked.

"Yeah."

"An' remember, when you find him, you murder his left mitt so he knows I ain't jokin'," Flip went on. "Don't touch his right hand. I need him to sign cheques and bank transfers." And he laughed.

But Doolan didn't join in. "This ain't funny, Mason. Anyone who's dissed my tiger is gonna get what's coming. Serious." He put his black helmet on, which made him look even more sinister.

"Good luck!" Flip said.

"Luck won't come into it!" Doolan's voice was muffled but loud. "Nineteen knock-outs from twenty-two championship bouts? *Good luck?*" He opened his throttle and was away, rattling shop windows on the way to the A2 and London.

*

"It's changed!" Sol said. "All we need!"

The notice-board told them that his old sixth-form college was now the Greenwich School of Cookery.

"They might still have your painting on a wall." Sofia tried to sound confident.

They went into the three-storey building to find Reception, and waited while a young woman spent ages on a phone call.

"Can I help you?" she asked at last, pleasant enough – but she couldn't help them. She told Sol that his college had been merged with Broadway Academy in Deptford and as far as she knew not much had gone down there from here. "It was skips in the street for a couple of weeks as they cleared stuff out," she told them.

Outside, Sofia stood and shook her head. "What vandals! How could a teacher who cared about art let your picture be thrown away? Didn't he care?"

"*She*. No, she would care, she was good." Sol's voice was serious. "And she was important to me, that woman. She saw me through a bad time." He looked both ways to cross the road. "Anyhow, let's get to Broadway. You never know, she might have transferred with the college."

They took a bus to Deptford Creek, walked from there and found themselves at a school that looked like a large 1970s greenhouse. There was so much glazing along the corridors it would have been hard to pin up a postcard let alone hang a picture.

Reception here was staffed by a young woman in a hijab. She was dealing with late arrivals and sent the students through the internal door as if they were going into youth custody. She listened to Sol's story. "That was a bit of time back," she said, and phoned an internal number. But after a short chat she said, "Nothing like that came along from Hyde."

"Can you tell me the name of your head of art?" Sol asked.

"Mr Toynbee. That was him on the phone," the receptionist replied.

"And do you have a Rachel Brunovsky on your staff?" Sol persisted.

The receptionist shook her head. "I'm not allowed to say."

"It's very important," Sofia said. "Sol painted a really beautiful picture of a tiger for his A Level, and he desperately wants to get it back – for very important personal reasons."

The receptionist looked at each of them and thought for a moment. "Shall I say Rachel Brunovsky is not a name that rings a bell?" she said. And that was that. She smiled politely and slid her window shut.

Well, Sofia thought, *she had been a help – in a negative way.*

Outside, Sol said, "Right, what do we do now?"

"Not give up." Sofia patted him on the back. "We find a library."

"A library?" Sol looked puzzled.

"We look up Rachel Brunovsky on the list of voters," Sofia explained.

"Agreed." He made Sofia smile. He'd said it as if it had been in his head all along. "Miss Brunovsky was local, she used to cycle to college."

"So we find out where she lives," Sofia said, then added, "and we hope she's still alive ..."

"Lord, I hadn't thought of that." Sol looked tense. "I need to be able to prove that picture is mine. A lot hangs on this," he said, and he held out his hands in front of Sofia. "Including these fingers and thumbs!"

"And that's too true to be funny," she said.

CHAPTER 8
The house in Maze Hill

With a great roar, the Ducati Monster pulled up near Covent Garden Tattoo. Tiger Doolan locked the motorbike, stowed his helmet and pushed his way into the building.

"Marks," he said to Annie. "I want Sol Marks." He looked around.

"He's not in today," Annie told him.

"Ain't he?" Doolan went up the stairs, threw open a couple of doors and clumped down again. "When's he coming back?"

Annie shrugged. "Tomorrow?"

"Know where he is?" Doolan stood with his feet apart like Henry the Eighth.

"He never said. But I'm afraid he's booked through to August ..."

"He won't be booked through to nuffin when I catch up with him!" Doolan growled, and he turned for the door so sharply that his heel splintered the floor. "Tell your guv'nor 'e'll be looking for a new tattoo boy tomorrer!" He went out, leaving Annie rolling her eyes in shock.

*

Back in Greenwich, Sol's phone blipped just as he and Sofia were in the local library being helped with the list of voters.

"Tiger's on your tail, Marks," the text read, "Say you're gonna pay an I'll call him off. Else you won't tattoo again. Ever."

Sol showed it to Sofia. "Flip Mason."

"Might this be the person you're seeking?" the librarian asked.

The electoral roll showed "Rachel Anne Brunovsky" against an address in Maze Hill, Greenwich.

"Could be her. I thought she was local. Thank you," Sol said. And to Sofia, "We'll get to Maze Hill, start at the bottom. I don't know how the house numbers run."

The librarian didn't know either, but they thanked him for his help and walked across the bottom of Greenwich Park, pushing on, not a word between them all the way. They came out at Maze Hill railway station and looked at the house numbers as they went up the hill. The houses were all on the left-hand side, opposite the wall of the park.

"She'll be near the top," Sol said. He led the way, away from the heavy sound of Greenwich traffic – cars, vans, buses and, coming closer, a big-engined heavy motorbike, so loud that it turned Sofia's head.

"Noise pollution!" she said. "What sort of person has to make a noise like that?"

*

The Ducati Monster had taken a left off Trafalgar Road and then a right. It had cruised along Greenwich Wharf Street, with Tiger Doolan checking off the numbers of the terraced houses. When he found number 32, he parked up, crossed the pavement and pressed the doorbell. There was no answer. He looked through the letterbox but it was masked. He stood back on the pavement and stared at the windows of the house. Nothing. Doolan turned back to his machine.

"Excuse me. Are you from Amazon? I'll take anything in for him," said an old woman who was passing.

Doolan looked at the woman, who was carrying a bag-for-life. "I live next door," she explained. "We take things in for one another. It's a friendly street."

"No, I want the guy," Doolan told her.

"Solomon. Mr Marks?" she checked.

"That's him."

"Well, I've just seen him, up past the shops," the woman told him. "He's with a young lady. By Maze Hill Station ..."

"Going for a train?" Doolan asked.

"No, walking up the hill. Probably going into the park." She chuckled.

But Doolan had climbed onto his motorbike and was roaring off.

"Must be an urgent message!" The old woman shook her head. "Could be life and death."

*

Sofia and Sol were standing outside a Maze Hill house built in Georgian style with a wide front door. It was much older than the houses lower down, and very stylish, set behind a sturdy brick wall.

"Looks about right," Sol said.

"Nice place," Sofia replied.

Sol opened the gate. "Let's get to it," he said.

They went up to the front door, which needed painting, and Sol pulled the old-fashioned bell. It jangled inside.

There was no answer. "I hope she's in," he said.

Just as Sol was about to pull the bell again, the door creaked. They both stepped back. Sol's face looked ready to greet Miss Brunovsky, and Sofia put on a pleasant smile.

The door swung open. Sofia saw Sol slump a little.

"Sorry. We were looking for Miss Brunovsky," he said.

"And you've found her." The woman was tall with a no-nonsense bearing. "Alice Brunovsky."

"But I'm looking for Miss *Rachel* Brunovsky," Sol said. "She used to teach me art ..."

Alice Brunovsky put on a mournful face. "Then I'm very sorry, but she's not here."

"Do you know when she might—" Sol began.

The woman shook her head, slowly and sadly. "I'm very sorry if you've wasted your time." She went to close the door – pulling an annoyed face at the sound of a powerful motorbike revving loudly down the hill – "I'm truly very sorry."

But Sofia had put her foot on the threshold. "Look!" she said, twisting Sol to see. There was Sol's painting, hanging on the wall of the entrance hall – a large colourful picture of the tiger with blue eyes. They'd found what they were searching for! *His* tiger! *Her* tiger!

"*That's* what we've come about!" Sofia cried out. "He painted it! This man here!"

"Ah!" said the woman. "Rachel's had it for years, loves it." Now she looked a little nervous, as if Sol and Sofia might have come to claim it back. "Well, if you're the artist, you have to know that you've given my sister and me much delight in recent years." She opened the door wider. "And he protects us."

She, thought Sofia.

"Do come in. Rachel will be so pleased when I tell her we've met."

Ah! So Rachel Brunovsky was still around …

"We can't talk out here with *that* racket going on." And Alice Brunovsky shut the door on the roar of a very large motorbike coming back the other way.

CHAPTER 9
Three Miss Brunovskys

Sol's eyes pulled away from his painting as Miss Brunovsky took them into the sitting room. They both refused coffee – time was too tight. But there was to be no hurrying her.

"I shall tell you about the painting, and my sister." She waved an arm for them to sit down and addressed herself to Sol. "Rachel brought the picture home from the college after it was clear that you weren't going to collect it. And after your father slammed his door in her face, she decided to keep it."

"I'm sorry about that." But Sol shot an anxious look at Sofia, then looked at his watch.

Sofia jumped in. "Someone is saying Sol didn't paint that picture. They're saying he didn't design that tiger, which is being used in a big film – and if he can't prove that he's the artist, the film company will take him to court," she explained.

"So I need to ask Miss Brunovsky to say that I painted that picture," Sol said. "That's the top and bottom of it."

Alice Brunovsky sighed. "Well, yes, and I'm sure she will. But it will be tricky to arrange. Rachel was diagnosed with something very nasty last year, and I'm afraid she's now in a hospice ..." Her voice remained firm.

"I'm so sorry," said Sol. Sofia murmured something too. "Could we borrow the painting, then?" Sol asked. "It should have all the proof I need stuck on the back."

"It has. But borrow it? I'm afraid not." Alice Brunovsky was very firm. "As far as I know, you might not be whom you say. And until that can be proven to Rachel's satisfaction, the painting must stay here."

The atmosphere in the room had chilled, but Sol took out his wallet. "I've got ID here, Miss Brunovsky, with a photo," he said.

"Which I must show to Rachel," Alice Brunovsky insisted. "She'll know you – there's nothing wrong with her mental faculties."

"Well, that's great!" Sol turned to Sofia with a bright face. "When can we go?" he asked.

"Oh, didn't I say? The hospice is in Worthing – and I shan't be visiting until the weekend."

Sol and Sofia sat there looking at one another. Stalemate. Until Sofia suddenly stood up. "Miss Brunovsky, would you be prepared to lend me one of your coats, and perhaps a beret?"

Alice Brunovsky looked out at the weather and frowned in confusion. It was warm and sunny.

"I've got an idea," Sofia went on. "If your phone is charged, Sol."

"Always." But he looked just as puzzled.

"Then if you agree, Miss Brunovsky, what we can do is this ..." And Sofia told them her plan to keep Flip Mason off Sol's back. They listened intently – while a beam of afternoon light came through the fanlight above the front door and lit up the face of the tiger in the hall.

Sofia stood in the sitting room dressed in a smart town coat and a black beret. She looked like an art expert taking a TV tour around an artist's house. She was in front of the settee with the tiger picture propped against it.

Sol held his mobile phone facing her and gave her the nod to start.

"I am here to tell you that the artist Solomon Marks painted this picture for his A Level examination, for which he received very good marks," Sofia said in a National Gallery guide voice. "The proof – the provenance – is on the reverse of the picture ..." She turned the picture around. "Here we see it."

Sol zoomed his phone camera in on the certificate pasted on the back:

UNIVERSITY OF LONDON EXAMINATION BOARD

Solomon Marks

BLUE-EYED TIGER

Hyde Sixth-Form College
Award: A*

Crispin Jenkins, Chief Examiner, Art and Design

Sofia read it aloud and carried on: "This is proof beyond any doubt that Solomon Marks is the creator of this artwork, 'Blue-eyed Tiger', and is the rightful owner of the picture and of its design." She turned the picture back to show the tiger staring out, matching her own stare into Sol's phone. She held the stare for a couple of beats and then called, "Cut!"

They had got the scene in one take. Tony Drake would have been very proud.

Sol immediately sent the clip to Flip Mason, as well as to Waterside Films and Tony Drake. "That'll do it," he said, as he hung the painting back in the hallway and took a picture of it. He turned to Alice Brunovsky. "When you see Miss Brunovsky, please thank her for everything she did for me – and tell her how pleased I am that she kept old blue-eyes. Wouldn't it be good if she could come home sometime to see it?"

"Thank you." But Alice Brunovsky shook her head sadly, as if that was very unlikely.

*

While Sofia had been giving her stellar performance, Tiger Doolan was prowling the streets. He rode his Ducati Monster to the top end of Maze Hill, into Greenwich Park and along to the Observatory at the far end. Now he took his helmet off and checked his picture of Sol Marks before he stared at the tourists and visitors all around. After watching for a while he gave up, cursing, then he revved out of the park and returned to the foot of Maze Hill. And there he sat, the machine ticking over like some growling beast, until he suddenly sat up to attention, opened his throttle wide and weaved in and out of the cars to head up Maze Hill.

"Gotcha!" he was saying inside his helmet. "Yes! Gotcha, my son!"

CHAPTER 10

A walk in the park?

Sol and Sofia were at the top of Maze Hill where it flattens out onto Blackheath. There were gorse bushes on their left, the park wall over the road on their right.

"I owe her a lot," Sol was saying. "Miss Brunovsky told me I was a good artist and she encouraged me. And she'd got this thing about tigers in art. Some Saturdays she'd take me up to the National Gallery to see Rousseau's tiger painting 'Surprised!' and a load of other stuff. She talked to me about tigers and their independence, how they live solitary lives and survive by their wits and skill. And in a weird way that made me feel better about being a bit solitary too. It helped make me single-minded, and I made damned sure I stayed at college and took my art exam before I called time on my dad."

"You're a bit like our tiger, then," Sofia said.

Sol turned to look at her. "And do you know – you're a bit like Rachel Brunovsky?"

"Oh? How?"

It took him a little while to say it, and he walked on as he did so. "Because you do me good, Sofe. Things are different when I'm with you."

Sofia couldn't think what to say to that, so she said nothing. Just felt it.

"And thanks for that ace idea back there." Sol lifted her hand and kissed it formally. Then, very matter-of-fact, he said, "I designed a red panda for you last night. Do you want to come back to my place and see it? I don't live far away."

Sofia opened her mouth to reply – just as the air was shaken by a beast of a motorbike that came roaring up at them. It mounted the footpath and blocked their way. The rider pulled off his helmet – a big man with a mean, battered face and hard eyes. "Gotcha!" he growled at Sol.

He took off his gauntlets and very deliberately laid his gear on his saddle.

Sofia had frozen. She looked in panic around her. Run this way? Run that?

"Make a move an' I'll mow you down!" The man shifted his feet and stood facing Sol. He slowly and deliberately started to crack his own knuckles, both hands, finger by finger. And when he'd finished, he said, "Give us that!", pointing to Sol's right hand. His tattooing hand.

Sofia couldn't think what to do. Kick at the man? Scratch his face? But Sol was standing there, calm and defiant. He flexed his right hand, but not to give it to the man, to get his phone out.

"Before you do something stupid, you look at this," Sol said. He flashed up a photograph. "There. The tiger."

Tiger Doolan squinted at what he was being shown.

"So what?" he growled.

"Do you see where it is?" Sol asked. "It's not on anyone's skin, it's not a tattoo. It's a painting, hanging on the wall in a lady's hallway, just down the road. I can take you there and she can tell you how long she's had it. Way before anything was ever done on your back."

Tiger Doolan looked at the photograph and frowned, then shook his head as if to clear it. And at that moment his own phone rang. He looked at the caller's name. "What d'you want, Mason?" he said into the phone. "I've got the geezer here. I was just going to work on him." But something Flip Mason said held him there, listening. And finally, with a hard stare at Sol, he switched off his phone.

"Mason's gonna take the hit," he said. "Which lets you off the hook, son. Says he got confused an' you *was* the one who done my tiger first."

"That's what I'm telling you," Sol said. "Mason had you over – he copied my design."

The man put his helmet and his gauntlets on and remounted his motorbike. He kick-started it and without another word he bumped off the pavement and headed towards the main road.

Sofia blew out a great sigh – but as she grabbed Sol's arm to get them away from there, the bike did a sudden skidding U-turn and raced back towards them. Sofia's insides turned over again.

The bike pulled up alongside them and the man's voice boomed through the visor of his helmet. "I just wanna say you done a good job, son. What's on my back – it's a terrific tattoo!"

And, dumbstruck, Sofia and Sol watched him ride off towards the A2 and Gravesend, leaving his exhaust fumes behind.

"Let's get some fresher air," Sol said. "The flower garden." He led the way into the park, where, in the calm between the flowerbeds, Sofia's shock and relief began to disperse amongst the springtime scents.

They walked the winding path and after a few metres Sofia said, "About that invitation to go back to your place and see my red panda ..."

"Yes?"

"Yes, please. I'd love to, if it's still on."

She smiled and linked her arm in his, and as they walked slowly through the park her left hand found Sol's right and laced itself between the artist's precious fingers.